HAUNTED HOUSES IN OR NEAR DUBLIN

BY
ST. JOHN D. SEYMOUR

British Library Cataloguing-in-Publication Data
A catalogue record for this book is available from the
British Library

CONTENTS

ST. JOHN D. SEYMOUR

St. John Drelincourt Seymour was born in the second half of the 19th century in Ireland. Around 1913, he came to realize that although Ireland was replete with collections of folklore and fairy-tales, the country's rich tradition of ghost stories remained largely untapped. Working with friend Harry L. Neligan, Seymour set out to correct this. The two of them put out a request for anecdotes in the newspapers of the day, and compiled the stories they received in what is now Seymour's most well-known 'non-fiction' work, True Irish Ghost Stories (1914). Around the same time, Seymour published his other more popular titles, Irish Witchcraft and Demonology and Haunted Houses in or Near Dublin.

TRUE IRISH GHOST STORIES

ST. JOHN D. SEYMOUR

HAUNTED HOUSES IN OR NEAR DUBLIN

OF all species of ghostly phenomena, that commonly known as "haunted houses" appeals most to the ordinary person. There is something very eerie in being shut up within the four walls of a house with a ghost. The poor human being is placed at such a disadvantage. If we know that a gateway, or road, or field has the reputation of being haunted, we can in nearly every case make a detour, and so avoid the unpleasant locality. But the presence of a ghost in a house creates a very different state of affairs. It appears and disappears at its own sweet will, with a total disregard for our feelings: it seems to be as much part and parcel of the domicile as the staircase or the hall door, and, consequently, nothing short of leaving the house or of pulling it down (both of these solutions are not always practicable) will free us absolutely from the unwelcome presence.

There is also something so natural, and at the same time so unnatural, in seeing a door open when we know that no human hand rests on the knob, or in hearing the sound of footsteps, light or heavy, and feeling that it cannot be attributed to the feet of mortal man or woman. Or perhaps a form appears in a room, standing, sitting, or walking—in fact, situated in its three dimensions apparently as an ordinary being of flesh and blood, until it proves its unearthly nature by vanishing before our astonished eyes. Or perhaps we are asleep in bed. The room is shrouded in darkness, and our recumbent attitude, together with the weight of bed-clothes, hampers our movements and probably makes us more cowardly. A man will meet pain or danger boldly if he be standing upright—occupying that erect position which is his as Lord of Creation; but his courage does not well so high if he be supine. We are awakened suddenly by the feel that some superhuman Presence is in the room. We are transfixed with terror, we cannot find either the bell-rope or the matches, while we dare not leap out of bed and make a rush for the door lest we should encounter we know not what. In an agony of fear, we feel it moving towards us; it approaches closer, and yet closer, to the bed, and—for what may or may not then happen we must refer our readers to the pages of this book.

But the sceptical reader will say: "This is all very well, but—there are no haunted houses. All these alleged strange happenings are due to a vivid imagination, or else to rats and mice." (The question of deliberate and conscious fraud may be rejected in almost every instance.) This simple solution has been put forward so often that it should infallibly have solved the problem long ago. But will such a reader explain how it is that the noise made by rats and mice can resemble slow, heavy footsteps, or else take the form of a human being seen by several persons; or how our imagination can cause doors to open and shut, or else create a conglomeration of noises which, physically, would be beyond the power of ordinary individuals to reproduce? Whatever may be the ultimate explanation, we feel that there is a great deal in the words quoted by Professor Barrett: "In spite of all reasonable scepticism, it is difficult to avoid accepting, at least provisionally, the conclusion that there are, in a certain sense, haunted houses, i.e. that there are houses in which similar quasi-human apparitions have occurred at different times to different inhabitants, under circumstances which exclude the hypothesis of suggestion or expectation."

We must now turn to the subject of this chapter. Mrs. G. Kelly, a lady well known in musical circles in Dublin, sends as her own personal experience the following tale of a most quiet haunting, in which the spectral charwoman (I) does not seem to have entirely laid aside all her mundane habits.

"My first encounter with a ghost occurred about twenty years ago. On that occasion I was standing in the kitchen of my house in —— Square, when a woman, whom I was afterwards to see many times, walked down the stairs into the room. Having heard the footsteps outside, I was not in the least perturbed, but turned to look who it was, and found myself looking at a tall, stout, elderly woman, wearing a bonnet and old-fashioned mantle. She had grey hair and a benign and amiable expression. We stood gazing at each other while one could Count twenty. At first I was not at all frightened, but gradually as I stood looking at her an uncomfortable feeling, increasing to terror, came over me. This caused me to retreat farther and farther back, until I had my back against the wall, and then the apparition slowly faded.

"This feeling of terror, due perhaps to the unexpectedness of her appearance, always overcame me on the subsequent occasions on which I saw her. These occasions numbered twelve or fifteen, and I have seen her in every room in the house, and at every hour of the day, during a period of about ten years. The last time she appeared was ten years ago. My husband and I had just returned from a concert at which he had been singing, and we sat for some time over supper, talking about the events of the evening. When at last I rose to leave the room, and opened the dining-room door, I found my old lady standing on the mat outside with her head bent towards the door in the attitude of listening. I called out loudly, and my husband rushed to my side. That was the last time I have seen her.

"One peculiarity of this spectral visitant was a strong objection to disorder or untidiness of any kind, or even to an alteration in the general routine of the house. For instance, she showed her disapproval of any stranger coming to sleep by turning the chairs face downwards on the floor in the room they were to occupy. I well remember one of our guests, having gone to his room one evening for something he had forgotten, remarking on coming downstairs again, 'Well, you people have an extraordinary manner of arranging your furniture! I have nearly broken my bones over one of the bedroom chairs which was turned down on the floor.' As my husband and I had restored that chair twice already to its proper position during the day, we were not much surprised at his remarks, although we did not enlighten him. The whole family have been disturbed by a peculiar knocking which occurred in various rooms in the house, frequently on the door or wall, but sometimes on the furniture, quite close to where we had been sitting. This was evidently loud enough to be heard in the next house, for our next-door neighbour once asked my husband why he selected such curious hours for hanging his pictures. Another strange and fairly frequent occurrence was the following. I had got a set of skunk furs which I fancied had an unpleasant odour, as this fur sometimes has; and at night I used to take it from my wardrobe and lay it on a chair in the drawing-room, which was next my bedroom. The first time that I did this, on going to the drawing-room I found, to my surprise, my muff in one corner and my stole in another. Not for a moment suspecting a supernatural agent, I asked my servant about it, and she assured me that she had not been in the room that morning. Whereupon I determined to test the matter, which I did by putting in the furs late at night, and taking care that I was the first to enter the room in the morning. I invariably found that they had been disturbed."

A most weird experience fell to the lot of Major Macgregor, and was contributed by him to Real Ghost Stories, the celebrated Christmais number of the Review of Reviews. He says: "In the end of 1871 I went over to Ireland to visit a relative living in a Square in the north side of Dublin. In January 1872 the husband of my relative fell ill. I sat up with him for several nights, and at last, as he seemed better, I went to bed, and directed the footman to call me if anything went wrong. I soon fell asleep, but some time after was awakened by a push on the left shoulder. I started up, and said, 'Is there anything wrong?' I got no answer, but immediately received another push. I got annoyed, and said, 'Can you not speak, man! and tell me if there is anything wrong?' Still no answer, and I had a feeling I was going to get another push when I suddenly turned round and caught a human hand, warm, plump, and soft. I said, 'Who are you?' but I got no answer. I then tried to pull the person towards me, but could not do so. I then said, 'I will know who you are!' and having the hand tight in my right hand, with my left I felt the wrist and arm, enclosed, as it seemed to me, in a tight-fitting sleeve of some winter material with a linen cuff, but when I got to the elbow all trace of an arm ceased. I was so astounded that I let the hand go, and just then the clock struck two. Including the mistress of the house, there were five females in the establishment, and I can assert that the hand belonged to none of them. When I reported the adventure, the servants exclaimed, 'Oh, it must have been the master's old Aunt Betty, who lived for many years in the upper part of that house, and had died over fifty years before at a great age.' I afterwards heard that the room in which I felt the hand had been considered haunted, and very curious noises and peculiar incidents occurred, such as the bedclothes torn off, etc. One lady got a slap in the face from some invisible hand, and when she lit her candle she saw as if something opaque fell or jumped off the bed. A general officer, a brother of the lady, slept there two nights, but preferred going to a hotel to remaining the third night. He never would say what he heard or saw, but always said the room was uncanny. I slept for months in the room afterwards, and was never in the least disturbed."

A truly terrifying sight was witnessed by a clergyman

in a schoolhouse a good many years ago. This cleric was curate of a Dublin parish, but resided with his parents some distance out of town in the direction of Malahide. It not infrequently happened that he had to hold meetings in the evenings, and on such occasions, as his home was so far away, and as the modern convenience of tramcars was not then known, he used to sleep in the schoolroom, a large bare room, where the meetings were held. He had made a sleeping-apartment for himself by placing a pole across one end of the room, on which he had rigged up two curtains which, when drawn together, met in the middle. One night he had been holding some meeting, and when everybody had left he locked up the empty schoolhouse and went to bed. It was a bright moonlight night, and every object could be seen perfectly clearly. Scarcely had he got into bed when be became conscious of some invisible presence. Then he saw the curtains agitated at one end, as if hands were grasping them on the outside. In an agony of terror he watched these hands groping along outside the curtains till they reached the middle. The curtains were then drawn a little apart, and a Face peered in—an awful, evil Face, with an expression of wickedness and hate upon it which no words could describe. It looked at him for a few moments, then drew back again, and the curtains closed. The clergyman had sufficient courage left to leap out of bed and make a thorough examination of the room, but, as he expected, he found no one. He dressed himself as quickly as possible, walked home, and never again slept a night in that schoolroom.

The following tale, sent by Mr. E. B. de Lacy, contains a most extraordinary and unsatisfactory element of mystery. He says: "When I was a boy I lived in the suburbs, and used to come in every morning to school, in the city. My way lay through a certain street in which stood a very dismal semi-detached house, which, I might say, was closed up regularly about every six months. I would see new tenants coming into it, and then in a few months it would be 'To let' again. This went on for eight or nine years, and I often wondered what was the reason. On inquiring one day from a friend, I was told that it had the reputation of being haunted.

"A few years later I entered business in a certain office, and one day it fell to my lot to have to call on the lady who at that particular period was the tenant of the haunted house. When we had transacted our business she informed me that she was about to leave. Knowing the reputation of the house, and being desirous of investigating a ghost-story, I asked her if she would give me the history of the house as far as she knew it, which she very kindly did as follows:

"About forty years ago the house was left by will to a gentleman named ——. He lived in it for a short time, when he suddenly went mad, and had to be put in an asylum. Upon this his agents let the house to a lady. Apparently nothing unusual happened for some time, but a few months later, as she went down one morning to a room behind the kitchen, she found the cook hanging by a rope attached to a hook in the ceiling. After the inquest the lady gave up the house.

"It was then closed up for some time, but was again advertised 'To let', and a caretaker, a woman, was put into it. One night about one o'clock, a constable going his rounds heard some one calling for help from the house, and found the caretaker on the sill of one of the windows holding on as best she could. He told her to go in and open the hall door and let him in, but she refused to enter the room again. He forced open the door and succeeded in dragging the woman back into the room, only to find she had gone mad.

"Again the house was shut up, and again it was let, this time to a lady, on a five-years' lease. However, after a few months' residence, she locked it up, and went away. On her friends asking her why she did so, she replied that she would rather pay the whole five years' rent than live in it herself, or allow any one else to do so, but would give no other reason.

" 'I believe I was the next person to take this house,' said the lady who narrated the story to me (i.e. Mr. de Lacy). 'I took it about eighteen months ago on a three years' lease, in the hopes of making money by taking in boarders, but

I am now giving it up because none of them will stay more than a week or two. They do not give any definite reason as to why they are leaving; they are careful to state that it is not because they have any fault to find with me or my domestic arrangements, but they merely say they do not like the rooms! The rooms themselves, as you can see, are good, spacious, and well lighted. I have had all classes of professional men; one of the last was a barrister, and he said that he had no fault to find except that he did not like the rooms! I myself do not believe in ghosts, and I have never seen anything strange here or elsewhere; and if I had known the house had the reputation of being haunted, I would never have rented it.' "

Marsh's library, that quaint, old-world repository of ponderous tomes, is reputed to be haunted by the ghost of its founder, Primate Narcissus Marsh. He is said to frequent the inner gallery, which contains what was formerly his own private library: he moves in and out among the cases, taking down books from the shelves, and occasionally throwing them down on the reader's desk as if in anger. However, he always leaves things in perfect order. The late Mr. ———, who for some years lived in the librarian's rooms underneath, was a firm believer in this ghost, and said he frequently heard noises which could only be accounted for by the presence of a nocturnal visitor; the present tenant is more sceptical.

The story goes that Marsh's niece eloped from the palace, and was married in a tavern to the curate of Chapelizod. She is reported to have written a note consenting to the elopement, and to have then placed it in one of her uncle's books to which her lover had access, and where he found it. As a punishment for his lack of vigilance, the Archbishop is said to be condemned to hunt for the note until he find it—hence the ghost.

The ghost of a deceased Canon was seen in one of the Dublin cathedrals by several independent witnesses, one of whom, a lady, gives her own experience as follows: "Canon —— was a personal friend of mine, and we had many times discussed ghosts and spiritualism, in which he was a profound believer, having had many supernatural experiences himself. It was during the Sunday morning service in the cathedral that I saw my friend, who had been dead for two years, sitting inside the communion-rails. I was so much astonished at the flesh-and-blood appearance of the figure that I took off my glasses and wiped them with my handkerchief, at the same time looking away from him down the church. On looking back again he was still there, and continued to sit there for about ten or twelve minutes, after which he faded away. I remarked a change in his personal appearance, which was, that his beard was longer and whiter than when I had known him—in fact, such a change as would have occurred

14

in life in the space of two years. Having told my husband of the occurrence on our way home, he remembered having heard some talk of an appearance of this clergyman in the cathedral since his death. He hurried back to the afternoon service, and asked the robestress if anybody had seen Canon ———'s ghost. She informed him that she had, and that he had also been seen by one of the sextons in the cathedral. I mention this because in describing his personal appearance she had remarked the same change as I had with regard to the beard."

Some years ago a family had very uncanny experiences in a house in Rathgar, and subsequently in another in Rathmines. These were communicated by one of the young ladies to Mrs. M. A. Wilkins, who published them in the Journal of the American S.P.R.,1 from which they are here taken. The Rathgar house had a basement passage leading to a door into the yard, and along this passage her mother and the children used to hear dragging, limping steps, and the latch of the door rattling, but no one could ever be found when search was made. The house-bells were old and all in a row, and on one occasion they all rang, apparently of their own accord. The lady narrator used to sleep in the back drawing-room, and always when the light was put out she heard strange noises, as if some one was going round the room rubbing paper along the wall, while she often had the feeling that a person was standing beside her bed. A cousin, who was a nurse, once slept with her, and also noticed these strange noises. On one occasion this room was given up to a very matter-of-fact young man to sleep in, and next morning he said that the room was very strange, with queer noises in it.

Her mother also had an extraordinary experience in the same house. One evening she had just put the baby to bed, when she heard a voice calling "mother". She left the bedroom, and called to her daughter, who was in a lower room, "What do you want?" But the girl replied that she had not called her; and then, in her turn, asked her mother if she had been in the front room, for she had just heard a noise as if some one was trying to fasten the inside bars of the shutters across. But her mother had been upstairs, and no one was in the front room. The experiences in the Rathmines house were of a similar auditory nature, i.e. the young ladies heard their names called, though it was found that no one in the house had done so.

Occasionally it happens that ghosts inspire a law-suit. In the seventeenth century they were to be found actively urging the adoption of legal proceedings, but in the nineteenth and twentieth centuries they play a more passive part. A case about a haunted house took place in Dublin in the year 1885, in which the ghost may be said to have won. A Mr. Waldron, a solicitor's clerk, sued his next-door neighbour, one Mr. Kiernan, a mate in the merchant service, to recover £500 for damages done to his house.

Kiernan altogether denied the charges, but asserted that Waldron's house was notoriously haunted. Witnesses proved that every night, from August 1884 to January 1885, stones were thrown at the windows and doors, and extraordinary and inexplicable occurrences constantly took place.

Mrs. Waldron, wife of the plaintiff, swore that one night she saw one of the panes of glass of a certain window cut through with a diamond, and a white hand inserted through the hole. She at once caught up a bill-hook and aimed a blow at the hand, cutting off one of the fingers. This finger could not be found, nor were any traces of blood seen.

A servant of hers was sorely persecuted by noises and the sound of footsteps. Mr. Waldron, with the aid of detectives and policemen, endeavoured to find out the cause, but with no success. The witnesses in the case were closely cross-examined, but without shaking their testimony. The facts appeared to be proved, so the jury found for Kiernan, the defendant. At least twenty persons had testified on oath to the fact that the house had been known to have been haunted.[1]

Before leaving the city and its immediate surroundings, we must relate the story of an extraordinary ghost, somewhat lacking in good manners, yet not without a certain distorted sense of humour. Absolutely incredible though the tale may seem, yet it comes on very good authority. It was related to our informant, Mr. D., by a Mrs. C., whose daughter he had employed as governess. Mrs. C., who is described as "a woman of respectable position and good education", heard it in her turn from her father and mother. In the story the relationship of the different persons seems a little involved, but it would appear that the initial A belongs to the surname both of Mrs. C.'s father and grandfather.

This ghost was commonly called "Corney" by the family, and he answered to this though it was not his proper name. He disclosed this latter to Mr. C.'s mother, who forgot it. Corney made his presence manifest to the A. family shortly after they had gone to reside in —— Street in the following manner. Mr. A. had sprained his knee badly, and had to use a crutch, which at night was left at the head of his bed. One night his wife heard some one walking on the lobby, thump, thump, thump, as if imitating Mr. A. She struck a match to see if the crutch had been removed from the head of the bed, but it was still there.

From that on Corney commenced to talk, and he spoke every day from his usual habitat, the coal-cellar off the kitchen. His voice sounded as if it came out of an empty barrel.

He was very troublesome, and continually played practical

jokes on the servants, who, as might be expected, were in terror of their lives of him; so much so that Mrs. A. could hardly induce them to stay with her. They used to sleep in a press-bed in the kitchen, and in order to get away from Corney, they asked for a room at the top of the house, which was given to them. Accordingly the press-bed was moved up there. The first night they went to retire to bed after the change, the doors of the press were flung open, and Corney's voice said, "Ha! ha! you devils, I am here before you! I am not confined to any particular part of this house."

Corney was continually tampering with the doors, and straining locks and keys. He only manifested himself in material form to two persons; to ———, who died with the fright, and to Mr. A. (Mrs. C.'s father) when he was about seven years old. The latter described him to his mother as a naked man, with a curl on his fore-head, and a skin like a clothes-horse (!).

One day a servant was preparing fish for dinner. She laid it on the kitchen table while she went elsewhere for something she wanted. When she returned the fish had disappeared. She there-upon began to cry, fearing she would be accused of making away with it. The next thing she heard was the voice of Corney from the coal-cellar saying, "There, you blubbering fool, is your fish for you!" and, suiting the action to the word, the fish was thrown out on the kitchen floor.

Relatives from the country used to bring presents of vegetables, and these were often hung up by Corney like Christmas decorations round the kitchen. There was one particular press in the kitchen he would not allow anything into. He would throw it out again. A crock with meat in pickle was put into it, and a fish placed on the cover of the crock. He threw the fish out.

Silver teaspoons were missing, and no account of them could be got, until Mrs. A. asked Corney to confess if he had done anything with them. He said, "They are under the ticking in the servants' bed." He had, so he said, a daughter in —— Street, and sometimes announced that he was going to see her, and would not be here tonight.

On one occasion he announced that he was going to have "company" that evening, and if they wanted any water out of the soft-water tank, to take it before going to bed, as he and his friends would be using it. Subsequently that night five or six distinct voices were heard, and next morning the water in the tank was as black as ink, and not alone that, but the bread and butter in the pantry were streaked with the marks of sooty fingers.

A clergyman in the locality, having heard of the doings of Corney, called to investigate the matter. He was advised by Mrs. A. to keep quiet, and not to reveal his identity, as being the best chance of hearing Corney speak. He waited a long time, and as the capricious Corney remained silent, he left at length. The servants asked, "Corney, why did you not speak?" and he replied, "I could not speak while that good man was in the house." The servants sometimes used to ask him where he was. He would reply, "The Great God would not permit me to tell you. I was a bad man, and I died the death." He named the room in the house in which he died.

Corney constantly joined in any conversation carried on by the people of the house. One could never tell when a voice from the coal-cellar would erupt into the dialogue. He had his likes and dislikes; he appeared to dislike any one that was not afraid of him, and would not talk to them. Mrs. C.'s mother, however, used to get good of him by coaxing. An uncle, having failed to get him to speak one night, took the kitchen poker, and hammered at the door of the coal-cellar, saying, "I'll make you speak"; but Corney wouldn't. Next morning the poker was found broken in two. This uncle used to wear spectacles, and Corney used to call him derisively, "Four-eyes". An uncle named Richard came to sleep one night, and complained in the morning that the clothes were pulled off him. Corney told the servants in great glee, "I slept on Master Richard's feet all night."

Finally Mr. A. made several attempts to dispose of his lease, but with no success, for when intending purchasers were being shown over the house and arrived at Corney's domain, the spirit would begin to speak and the would-be purchaser would fly. They asked him if they changed house would he trouble them. He replied, "No! but if they throw down this house, I will trouble the stones."

At last Mrs. A. appealed to him to keep quiet, and not to injure people who had never injured him. He promised that he would do so, and then said, "Mrs. A., you will be all right now, for I see a lady in black coming up the street to this house, and she will buy it." Within half an hour a widow called and purchased the house. Possibly Corney is still there, for our informant looked up the Directory as he was writing, and found the house marked "Vacant".

Near Blanchardstown, Co. Dublin, is a house, occupied at present, or up to very recently, by a private family; it was formerly a monastery, and there are said to be secret passages in it. Once a servant ironing in the kitchen saw the figure of a nun approach the kitchen window and look in. Our informant was also told by a friend (now dead), who had it from the lady of the house, that once night falls, no doors can be kept closed. If any one shuts them, almost immediately they are flung open again with the greatest violence and apparent anger. If left open there is no trouble or noise, but light footsteps are heard, and there is a vague feeling of people passing to and fro. The persons inhabiting the house are matter-of-fact, unimaginative people, who speak of this as if it were an everyday affair. "So long as we leave the doors unclosed they don't harm us: why should we be afraid of them?" Mrs. —— said. Truly a most philosophical attitude to adopt!

A haunted house in Kingstown, Co. Dublin, was investigated by Professor W. Barrett and Professor Henry Sidgwick. The story is singularly well attested (as one might expect from its being inserted in the pages of the Proceedings S.P.R.1), as the apparition was seen on three distinct occasions, and by three separate persons who were all personally known to the above gentlemen. The house in which the following occurrences took place is described as being a very old one, with unusually thick walls. The lady saw her strange visitant in her bedroom. She says: "Disliking cross-lights, I had got into the habit of having the blind of the back window drawn and the shutters closed at night, and of leaving the blind raised and the shutters opened towards the front, liking to see the trees and sky when I awakened. Opening my eyes now one morning, I saw right before me (this occurred in July 1873) the figure of a woman, stooping down and apparently looking at me. Her head and shoulders were wrapped in a common woollen shawl; her arms were folded, and they were also wrapped, as if for warmth, in the shawl. I looked at her in my horror, and dared not cry out lest I might move the awful thing to speech or action. Behind her head I saw the window and the growing dawn, the looking-glass upon the toilet-table, and the furniture in that part of the room. After what may have been only seconds—of the duration of this vision I cannot judge—she raised herself and went backwards towards the window, stood at the toilet-table, and gradually vanished. I mean she grew by degrees transparent, and that through the shawl and the grey dress she wore I saw the white muslin of the table-cover again, and at last saw that only in the place where she had stood." The lady lay motionless with terror until the servant came to call her. The only other occupants of the house at the time were her brother and the servant, to neither of whom did she make any mention of the circumstance, fearing that the former would laugh at her, and the latter give notice.

Exactly a fortnight later, when sitting at breakfast, she noticed that her brother seemed out of sorts, and did not eat. On asking him if anything were the matter, he answered, "I have had a horrid nightmare—indeed it was no nightmare: I saw it early this morning, just as distinctly as I see you." "What?" she asked. "A villainous-looking hag," he replied, "with her head and arms wrapped in a cloak, stooping over me, and looking like this——" He got up, folded his arms, and put himself in the exact posture of the vision. Whereupon she informed him of what she herself had seen a fortnight previously.

About four years later, in the same month, the lady's married sister and two children were alone in the house. The eldest child, a boy of about four or five years, asked for a drink, and his mother went to fetch it, desiring him to remain in the dining-room until her return. Coming back she met the boy pale and trembling, and on asking him why he left the room, he replied, "Who is that woman—who is that woman?" "Where?" she asked. "That old woman who went upstairs," he replied. So agitated was he, that she took him by the hand and went upstairs to search, but no one was to be found, though he still maintained that a woman went upstairs. A friend of the family subsequently told them that a woman had been killed in the house many years previously, and that it was reported to be haunted.

A lady sends a very curious account of the appearance of an archiepiscopal ghost in a house in the outskirts of Dublin. Those of my readers who are acquainted with that Archbishop's family history will be able to say if some of the facts related below are correct.

A good many years ago a Mrs. P., an intimate friend of the narrator, lived in Upper Fitzwilliam Street. Her husband had held the post of Government arbitrator, and was subsequently agent to a large estate. During his lifetime he and his wife resided at a house near Dundrum, Co. Dublin, a great rambling old mansion, which has since suffered the fate of so many stately houses, as it has become a teaching establishment of some sort.

One afternoon, when it was getting dusk, Mrs. P. was descending the large staircase when she saw going down before her what she imagined to be her youngest son, W., curiously attired. She had three sons, all of whom were very fond of amateur theatricals, and from the dress that W. wore she thought that he was about to take part in some rehearsal. He was clad in a large broad-brimmed sombrero, and a cloak put on in Spanish fashion. She called to him by name, bidding him wait for her, but to her surprise he took absolutely no notice, but continued descending, she following him, until he reached the door of the dining-room, which he entered. She was quite annoyed at his want of manners, and followed him into the dining-room, an apartment which they did not always use because it was very large. To her utter astonishment she found herself confronted, not by her son, but by an utter stranger who had walked to the far side of the dining-table, and there stood facing her. His cloak was pulled up so as to cover his mouth, and his hat drawn well down over his face, and on this account Mrs. P. was unable to distinguish his features, but she could see that his eyes were looking at her. Then he walked a little round the table, and suddenly vanished. Mrs. P. got a great shock, but her sons, when they heard it, attributed it to imagination pure and simple.

"I had heard this story many times, and never paid much heed to it," continued our narrator. ' 'However, one day I went to a Loreto Convent to visit some nuns of my acquaintance who were there for their holidays, and while there the conversation turned on the subject of ghosts. I related the story I have just told to you. One of the nuns present asked if she might bring in another nun to hear the story; this latter was a Rev. Mother of an English House who was over for her holiday. I was quite agreeable, so this Rev. Mother was introduced, and to her I told my tale again. She seemed more than usually interested, and said she would particularly like to meet Mrs. P., if it were possible, and would I ask her to try and recall the exact day and date on which she had seen the figure in the dining-room.

"I made an arrangement with Mrs. P., and brought her to the convent, where she met this Rev. Mother, to whom she related her experience, giving day and date, and almost the exact hour. From the subsequent conversation I learnt that this Rev. Mother was a niece, or some near relative, of the celebrated Archbishop Whately; she had turned Roman Catholic, and had entered a Loreto Convent. The Archbishop had owned this old mansion where Mrs. P. had lived, and had resided there for some time. It was said that he used to appear there whenever any near relative of his died. On ascertaining the day and date of the appearance to

Mrs. P., the Rev. Mother was able to say that exactly at that time her cousin, a daughter (I think) of the Archbishop's, had passed away. He had been in Spain, and had brought back from there the sombrero and cloak which he fancied very much. Thus the theatrically-clad figure which was seen by my friend was none other than the Archbishop himself."

A much more unpleasant haunting was experienced by Mrs. E.H.B. and her daughters in a house on the south side of Dublin.[1]

"This house was a large, sunny, rambling old place, not the least like the typical 'haunted house'. Our two girls occupied a very large room at the back of the house, little F. being a hopeless invalid, and needing some one to sleep in her room.

"We had been there about a week, and we had just gone to bed, when M. (our eldest girl) rushed wildly into our room crying: 'Mother, there is something rushing about in our bedroom, and we can't see it, and F. is so frightened—do come!'

"I ran down at once, and on the stairs I could distinctly hear something jumping about in their room, the door of which was open. Before we got in, however, the noise stopped, but I promised I would stay with them all night, for poor little F. could not speak, and clung to me convulsively.

"At last all was quiet, the girls slept, when I heard in one corner of the room a soft, sighing, whispering sound, which seemed to come out of the wall, and gradually crept all round the room till it reached where our beds were. Nearer it came, till it touched the bed, as if a winged beetle were fluttering against the quilt. All at once something heavy seemed to fall, and immediately the footfalls I had heard before sounded with a peculiar hollow thud, as if some animal (cat or dog) were jumping up and down; it lasted about ten minutes, and suddenly died away at the door. Next morning both girls exactly described the first part of the noise as I had heard it, and it always came in the same way—an indescribable whisper in the beginning, and the conclusion a heavy thud.

"But next day we had a visit from a friend (!), a pet aversion of ours, whose presence always put little sensitive F. into a fever. I subsequently noticed that whenever this person came to see us we always received a visit overnight from the 'Pronc' (a name that F. gave to the 'thuddy' sounds of our ghost), as if it knew that some evil was on its way to us, and was drawn to the spot by its magnetic influence. Indeed after a visit from the 'Pronc' I always stayed in next day to be on the spot and protect the children.

"One evening I was sitting in the firelight by F.'s bed, telling her stories, as I often did, when she gripped my hand, and nodded towards the fire. I looked round. There on the rug, with its back to us, sat a black animal, like a large tomcat, gazing into the fire! I thought it was F.'s pet cat, and called out, 'Well, Peter-Puss! Are you come in for your supper?' The creature turned, and looked full at us for a moment with eyes that were human, and a face which, though black, was still the face of an ugly woman! The mouth snarled at us for an instant, and a sad, angry howl came from it; and as we stared in horror, the thing vanished. We never saw it again, but the strain was too much, and we left the house as soon as we could. We were told later that fifty years before a woman had been robbed and murdered in that room by her son, and buried by him under the hearthstone! Twenty years after, her skeleton was found by tenants, who, troubled by the ghost, searched the house, and gave their gruesome find decent burial."

1 For September 1913,

1 See Sights and Shadows, p. 42 ff.

1 July 1884, p. 141.

1 Occult Review, vol. iii. p; 19.